HEART AND BLOOD

To my nieces

I am so proud of the amazing young women you are becoming. I wish you strength to overcome all obstacles, and I hope you find peace and happiness throughout your journey.

Contents

THE BEGINNING

Heart and Blood is the tale of a warrior, destined to overcome the evil in the world. Diane's journey begins humbly, quietly, as she abandons all she thought was dear to her. Follow her as she and the bard share her story of victory, love, and loss.

HEART AND BLOOD

Whether from dreams or truth
Warriors begin alone
Sorrow haunts their legends
Solitude is their home

Many songs and tales rise
Most with a hint of fact
Drawn to them we may be
Danger appears to lack

Love is most often lost
Light is disregarded
Heed the words of this bard
Hide and be not scarred

The Bard

COVER

Cover me with peace
Betray my warrior's nature
Love the lonely spirit
Free me from life of peril

Fate has yet to call
Battles yet I have not fought
Time passes in the calm
With worry my mind is fraught

Destiny appeals
She pleads to consume my soul
I know I shall relent
Blood shall discover its role

Harmony is done
My stories now shall unfold
So cover me with peace
And shelter me from the cold

The Warrior

QUEST

Moonlight streams through the window to the room
Illuminating with its stealthy glow
While Diane sits at peace there in the gloom
Wondering at those things she may not know

Not quite sad, though maybe in denial
She begs the answers of the pale wise moon
He looks down and gives her a solemn smile
As if to say; "Answers will come too soon."

She glides out to be bathed in his soft light
Turns her face to him, eyes closed, hands extended,
Ears tuned, listening for his sound insight
Concerning what nature has intended

Long minutes pass and all that she can hear
Are hoots and chirps and a distant long growl;
The sweet soft bubbling of the stream so near
And almost too close – a lonely wolf's howl.

She opens her eyes and shouts to the stars
Pleading for reply, be it foul or fair.
Gods she beseeches, even angry Mars
For the least response that any would share.

Hearing nothing but the sounds of the dark
Diane sinks; the earth feels a single tear.
The Mother sends music from dawn's first lark
With the intention to brighten and cheer.

The sun begins to show his golden face
Diane now doubts that nature cares at all
She begins to mourn for the human race
On her deaf ear, the replies could not fall.

The Bard

THE END

The man sits, waiting
Extends his hand, expecting
Knowing his wants, pleading
Unwilling to try, begging

She walks out, leaving
Closes the door, departing
Knowing her needs, refusing
Not giving in, ceasing

The Bard

THE CROWDS

People pushing past
Words will themselves to my ear
I will not listen

The Warrior

Alone

She walks through the forest
Unencumbered with pride
Tears and dust stain her face
From pain, she cannot hide

Life is not worth living
The moon looks on in grief
Soft light he shines for her
Not melting her belief

Unaware, unchanging
Blinded to the beauty
She sinks to the soft ground
Knowing not her duty

Grasses her only pillow
Shelter only the trees
Sleeping through her sorrow
Warmed by the sweet soft breeze

The Bard

SURVIVAL

Through sorrow and spite
I won a victory tonight
The wounds gently began to heal
As tears slowed their spill

Life itself may sting
Yet it may still be worth living
Though the world may have a steep cost
I may not be lost

To the woods I'll keep
And to the peaceful waters deep
The pain of others will prey
So away I'll stay

The Warrior

FORESTS

Serenity
Peace
Quiet

In the forest, these things I find
Through the fields, the feelings unwind

Tranquility
Harmony
Silence

Away from the city, these things I cherish
Away from the crowds, my thoughts I relish

The Warrior

HEART OF A WARRIOR

As Diane learns to be content with her life in the wilderness, she also discovers its dangers. She must learn to defend herself – and eventually others – from the threats of both man and beast.

The Awakening

Awake
Startled
Cold and alone
Searching the dark

Soft sounds
Probing
Steps and whispers
Looting the gear

Silent
Afraid
Waiting for peace
Mourning lost goods

Moonlight
Starlight
Revealed faces
Smiling at greed

Anger
Righteous
Terrible deed
Thieves cannot win

Moving
Reaching
Forgotten branch
Now in her hand

Silent
Lethal
Burglars shall lose
Dead at her feet

The Bard

THE STORM

Somehow I can't get warm
As I stand in the storm
Rain all about me
Wind all around me
Clouds all above me

I shiver from the cold
Come inside, I've been told
Rain soaking through me
Wind shrieking to me
Clouds calling to me

I've no need to get warm
I'm a part of the storm
Rain falling from me
Wind blowing in me
Clouds a part of me

The Warrior

MOONLIGHT

She creeps
Under the spell of the shadows
Ridding
Her home of villains who impose
Sunlight
Is no longer her welcome friend
Blinding
Days of brightness are at an end
The moon
Shields and guards her as she conquers
The cave
Keeps and hides her as she slumbers

The Bard

ARISEN

Ancient sword in moonlight
Lately purchased
Examined and practiced
Polished and bright

Thieves no longer bother
Disturbing sleep
Seeing the cold gleam they run
Passing over

Nearby a woman screams
Our lass searches
Finds the source of the wail
Disturbed by pain

Fighting the crowd she runs
Sword drawn, ready
Finds the man who would harm
Metal on his neck

Struggling he turns
Grabbing the sword she holds
Her fear is plain
Though her mission is fixed

Twisting the blade
Thrusting it into his arm
Resolved to win
Blood covering her hand

Running in pain
Embarrassed at defeat
This man is crushed
Never to harm again

The Bard

Aiding

Child running in fear
Mother anxiously searching
Father sobs in grief

Champion arrives
Searching out the beast
Facing snow and rain

The monster is found
Slaughtered with cold abandon
Children returned home

Parents rejoicing
Turning to thank the victor
She cannot be found

The Bard

WOLF AND MOON

Blood courses through her veins
She feels the throbbing in her neck
Head
Hands
Everywhere

The wolf stands, teeth dripping blood
Not hers; she sees the innocent victim
Dying
Weeping
Turning cold

A cloud passes over the moon, dulling the light
She sees only the yellow eyes – a step closer
Closer
Stopping
Staring

The moon returns, and the wolf howls
AAAAooooooooooo
Her blood runs faster, hair stands on end
Pulsing
Burning
Alive

She grips the knife harder, wondering if it will be enough
She looks up at the wolf, watching the slow movement towards her
Tensed
Anxious
Ready

The wolf runs, growling, pouncing
She rushes to meet him, a battle cry forcing itself from her lips
She stabs
He bites
Pain

They clash, his teeth and claws tearing her skin
Her knife rips his fur, piercing the thick skin
Minutes
Hours
Unending

They both tire, but neither will relent
The wolf pants, she sees her moment, thrusting the knife
Neck
Blood
Warmth

The wolf makes a last snap toward her hand, but he is slowing
He drifts to the ground, next to his last victim as she feels new energy,
stabbing again
Death
Pity
Victory

The Bard

Rebirth of Love

Though Diane has resolved to protect the innocent, she starts to feel the solitude of the life she has chosen and aches for companionship. She overlooks her yearning to accept the destiny the moon has silently shown her – to be the champion of the gods – but is found by another who promises a more tranquil and sun-filled path.

TWISTED

Brown water reflects
The dark snow-covered branches
As the waves twist them

The Bard

SEARCHING

I cling tight to thoughts of my former life
Though I hold to the new strength of this knife
Visions call out from the lonely distance
Driving my soul to higher existence

Thoughts well of the victor's life I designed
Solitude encases a wanderer's mind
Through the bitter cold and dark I must fight
Never caring that I hide from the bright light

Moon, far away, is my constant ally
Changing nightly, shining ever brightly
Prodding me to follow relentless dreams
I accept the quest beneath his kind beams

The Warrior

MIST

The mist closes
Clouding the path so I cannot see
I look behind and see only fog
I look ahead and see only fear
I linger
Cautious
Testing each dear step

The fog thickens
I cannot see; my hands are hidden
I look left and see only nothing
I look right and see only despair
I stop
Waiting
Sinking to the ground

The vapor holds
I cannot think; my mind is empty
I reflect past and feel only nothing
I judge future and sense only shade
I cry
Broken
Yielding to the end

I hear a voice
I cannot make out words or visage
I listen behind and hear no one
I listen ahead and perceive hope
I stand
Waiting
Watching through the haze

I see a face
I cannot recognize the features
Though it seems he's found the path ahead
I feel ahead and sense no evil
I feel ahead and sense no kindness
I walk
Guarded
Waiting for a sign

I hear a sound
I see the face and it's beautiful
I feel around and sense the evil
I feel around and sense the hatred
I'm pushed
Drowning
Waiting for the end

The Warrior

DROWNING

Water, covering the blood-soaked body
Washes away all traces of battle
Heavy gleaming sword sinks to the white sand
Peace longed for at last may be bitter won

To the stars she may be pulled now to rest
Though the flesh will drift with the changing waves
Simple steps and missteps may lead her on
To the peace the clash of iron could not

Troubled eyes close as sun melts heavy fog
Relinquishing endless wars for sweet death
No last deep breath of air will come to her
No noble warrior's proper departure

Settling to silt near her mighty weapon
Lovely, though nearing sweetly tragic end
Tender hands reaching down find her quickly
Pulling her to the shore's solid safety

Ensuring health for now and near future
The tall man turns promptly and walks away
Another arrives and wakes the victor
Carries her away from the water's edge

The Bard

Despair

Often we despair
Many setbacks block our path
Slowly we move on

The Bard

Revival

Moonlight caresses her face
As she contemplates calm seas
Death looked away in disgrace

Arisen and again free
The phoenix survives once more
To be as she needs to be

The Bard

MEETING

New city, new face
Mild, fair, and mysterious
Love at first meeting

The Bard

RESISTANCE

Daring to combat the strong will to fight
I stay with this calm man I now call Love
There is nothing more pleasing to my sight
Than my own companion sent from above

I rise with the sun and sleep with the moon
And he calls to me from the sandy shore
Though the moon beckons me to join him soon
And I lust for old thrills I seek no more

There is nothing like the passion so sweet
And the bittersweet call to rest my head
Though without drifting I feel not complete
And seek to feel my soul without that dread

I rightly choose comfort and my darling
Content to peace with the water sparkling

The Warrior

VISION

Clanging awakens her from deep slumber
Trinkets tumble
Endless apparitions call from the night
Demands are drowned

Light streams in through a forgotten window
Moonbeams beckon
She stares longingly at the shining stars
Closes curtains

Dreams appeal her return to the mission
Duty demands
Spirits reach out to her through a deep sleep
Linger longer

The Bard

Fear

Positive of nothing
Trembling with doubt
Bravery dead
Nothingness fills my soul

Dying from fear and pain
I would rather face a thousand dragons
Than face one moment in my mind
I cannot sleep because I think
I cannot wake because I dream

Physical fear is not fear
The fear of you drowns me
Broken, doubting my own senses
If I should die, know that I love you
Your pain, my pain
Your joy, mine

The Warrior

MY OWN

His stare reminds me that I am no longer my own
Though I cannot give all of myself to him
My own life for his I would willingly give
And torture for his comfort I would gladly endure

I did not want or wish to feel these feelings again
My heart of ice would not melt a second time
My own fears protected the life I treasured
And the surface, impenetrable, let no one in

But one moment in his arms and my own walls weakened
His touch traversed the bridge in a mere instant
His powerful eyes seemed a ram at the gate
He stands firm, waiting for the damaged walls to crumble

My own life without him I now cannot imagine
But cannot conceive life completely with him
My soul is torn, choosing between the two paths
Brings a burden that I would never have wished to bear

So for now, I choose to not make a choice of my own
Anticipating the one clearly laid path
Never voicing the wondrous things that I feel
Never voicing the uncertainty in my own mind

The Warrior

LOVE'S DEATH

Fighting a losing battle;
One I cannot win.
The voice of the one who calls me
Ends in eternal sin.
The loves that life can offer
Pale everlasting to him.

I wait and hope
And lie within
Trying, ever trying
For it to happen
Knowing, ever knowing
He will never give in.

I walk, knowing, into the lion's den.

The Warrior

TODAY

All past ever wants
Is to be history, to
Disappear in mist

All the present wants
Is what IS, nothing more; past,
Past; future unknown

All the future wants
Is to be left to the fates,
Mysterious now

The Bard

Invincible
Incredible
Unstoppable

I feel high
I can fly
I walk to the edge
Looking down
Two thousand miles
No fear
No danger
On top of the world

I jump
I fall
Hopeless
Realistic
Destructible

I find the wind
I soar
Rising up
To the top
No worries
No grief
Above the top of the world

I rise
To the sun
Powerful
Ecstatic
Effervescent
I feel pain
The sun scorches

I lose the airstream
Plummeting
Seeming forever
Panic
Perilous

The Warrior

MESSENGER

The messenger is my ruler
The thief, my mentor
My guide, the traveler

My love is the air around me
Death cannot claim me
Change does not trouble me

Creation springs from my small hand
Dreams cannot be spanned
Fancy lives in my mind

Happiness is ever-present
Verse can be written
Never cause to repent

Your creation cannot be scorned
Your thoughts uncensored
Right or wrong, they are owned

The Warrior

DESTINY'S CALL

Diane has resolved to give up her past and along with it, the victories fate has assured would be hers. In its place, she embraced a peaceful and creative life in the light of day with her love. The gods, however, have different plans, and their demands to fulfil her destiny grow more urgent.

SUN AND SHADOW

The green leaf sparkles
Another lies in shadow
As the sun shines down

The Bard

CALLING

Mother Earth calls out
Her hero must be returned
No longer a choice

The Bard

YIELDING

The fates cry out
Demanding that I go on
The furies scream
Never minding the dawn

My path is set
I can no longer refuse
My will be cursed
I must now pay my dues

I choose to go
Their call must be satisfied
Reprieve I leave
To the unknown I stride

The Warrior

ENDLESS LADDER

I step up to another rung
As my hand moves to the next
My arms are tired
My hands throb with splinters

The pine turns to oak as I climb
I stare up but see no end
No rest in sight
But I slowly move on

I finally see a landing
Far up as the wood darkens
I climb faster
Fall onto the soft rug

People sit and chat as I sleep
Partying and relaxing
I wake and sit
Determined to move on

I step on the endless ladder
Steadily climbing again
Still determined
Lonely, but positive

The Warrior

CHOICES

The Gods have gathered around
My choice is now to be made
Evil at last must be fought
The price is soon to be paid

Tempted to hide in shadow
Drawn to the world once again
Love cries out for a moment
Fear of what could be my bane

Obliged by fate and heaven
I turn to the Gods to plea
Sadly their heads are shaking
No other path can they see

Not a soul can force my hand
My will must be chosen now
To run or to face the foe
To cower or keep my vow

I cannot return coward
I cannot see the disgrace
Win or lose, fail or triumph
The next hurdle must I face

The Warrior

LOST

Lost in a world of hate
Enclosed with frozen darkness
Chosen by self and fate
Narrowed by her steadfastness

A thousand worlds cannot hold the bitter chill
A thousand hells cannot contain the burning evil
A thousand heavens cannot transfigure the hateful demon

Fate has chosen the day
Destruction will surely come
Wicked or good must pay
Though neither can guess the sum

A thousand worlds cannot grasp the bitter love
A thousand hells cannot alter the burning pity
A thousand heavens cannot embrace the hateless purity

With a frightening roar
The dreaded battle begins
Equipped with shining swords
Blades clash and sweetly sing

Calmness overtakes her
As she takes her final strike
Heaven is the victor
The sun emerges bright

A thousand worlds cannot face the bitter joy
A thousand hells cannot rejoice the burning disgust
A thousand heavens cannot encompass the hateful relief

Kneeling she sheds a tear
Captive though freed from above
Named Evil's Destroyer
Cursed, for that monster was her love

The Bard

ANGUISH

Tears stream down
I cannot see
I cannot know
How it can be

The Warrior

GRAY

Each day is grayer than the previous
Each nightfall darker than the blackest hell
Every thought is of the one I have lost
Every dream, misery I cannot quell

Tears, ever present, wet my pale cold cheeks
The laughter I knew in another life
Teases when I think of my fearsome deeds
The cold constantly reminds of this strife

Many moons may pass before my heart heals
My life is over, never to return
Many days of this anguish I will feel
My nights are full of heartache while I yearn

Though the light is still there; I cannot see
Until I launch a search beyond the sea

The Warrior

An Everlasting Quest

Diane has defeated the threatened evil and is now the heroine she was always meant to be. Her loss is the world's gain. In her misery, the gods see fit to find mercy as they request that she undertake one last mission and return to the night.

COMPASSION

The Gods have seen
And they have heard
The pain you endure

The Gods have felt
And they have known
The dark you were dealt

The Gods still grieve
And they still grasp
The sting of your loss

The Gods still learn
And they still aid
The hurt you now feel

The Gods still care
And they still share
The gifts they can give

The Bard

Light Shines Again

I felt a small still light through the window
Of the home of sorrow and bitter pain
My tears burned as I slipped into limbo
They left a thin, wet meandering stain

The light grew stronger in my small chamber
My cries lessened as the beams warmed my cheek
Though to my small realm I seemed a savior
A deliverer myself I did seek

The agony felt seemed distant and cold
For the soft light warmed my heart as I wept
A visage appeared in the dark so bold
Then through the open door tranquilly swept

Comfort found me as he walked down the hall
For the man had been with me through it all

The Warrior

THE MOON

Gentle moon sees all
Protecting from deepest night
His light out of love

The Bard

LOVE'S REALIZATION

He was always there
I never knew
He was always there
I never thought

He always loved me
I never knew
He always loved me
I never thought

I was always there
He always knew
I always loved him
He always thought

I always loved him
He always knew
I always loved him
He always thought

The Warrior

PURITY

To be loved so true
I never rightly knew
A sweetness so pure
A draught of sorrow's cure
The kiss I now seek
Causes knees to be weak
Gladness is my vow
Never furrows my brow

The Warrior

THE NIGHT

Night's invitation came long ago
Following her for so long
No notice she gave to the soft glow
Of his lovely patient song

However now evidence is clear
She returns to gentle night
Returns willing and with cheer
Ever bathing in his light

Love without pain is much more fair
She knows now how it can be
Forever now, midnight she will share
And her heart, joyful will be

The Bard

HONEYMOON

The gods look down in perfect harmony
Smiling upon the beauty from above
Joyful their lonely brother finally
Has now found his long-awaited true love

A feast the world has rarely ever seen
Rains on the unknowing people below
Water and wine and all delicacies
The gods adorn sky with colorful bows

As the groom with his bride set to wander
The dark lovely starlit honeymoon path
Nights together they never will squander
Never to suffer the deities' wrath

Never alone will the two lovers be
For each other they will forever see

The Bard

MOON'S BRIDE

Moon's bride always near
Travelling the skies above
Smiling down on Earth

When night is unlit
Moon and bride travel the land
Look to meet the foe

Mighty battles win
Then return home to the sky
Gentle 'til next time

The Bard

LOVING THE MOON

I love the moon
With his gentle face
For him I swoon
From his home in space
To him I sing
For his tender glow
To light I cling
And I feel no woe

The Warrior

Through unnumbered obstacles
Lost love and bitter death
The lone warrior persevered

Her tales through me now are done
I know no more to tell
Her fight on earth is finished

Still in heaven, quests are led
Some sent to mortals here
Her labor is never done

The Bard

IMMORTAL

The light I sought with mortals here
Has reached an end at last
My love has never left me
Though thwarted, he held fast

No regrets are found in my soul
Nothing would change my past
The battles won and lost are yours
To be told if you ask

I leave for where my heart is free
My longings are no more
Seek the same in all you may find
Look for the open door

The Warrior

ABOUT THE AUTHOR

Amelia has been writing for most of her life. Her first novel, *The Sanctity of Marriage*, was published in early 2025, and she has additional works in progress. She lives in northwest Georgia with her family and pets and loves creating artistically, especially through the written word.

www.ingramcontent.com/pod-product-compliance
Lightning Source LLC
Chambersburg PA
CBHW010738100726
47899CB00009B/3100